For Oliver

There are days when Bartholomew is naughty, and other days when he is very very good.

First published 2001 by Walker Books Ltd, 87 Vauxhall Walk, London SE11 5HJ

© 2001 Virginia Miller

This book has been typeset in Garamond.

Printed in Belgium

British Library Cataloguing in Publication Data
A catalogue record for this book is available from the British Library.

ISBN 0-7445-7551-6

IN A MINUTE!

Virginia Miller

WALKER BOOKS

AND SUBSIDIARIES

LONDON • BOSTON • SYDNEY

George was carrying logs.
Bartholomew wanted to play.
"In a minute, Ba," said George.
"When I've finished,
then we'll play."

George was hanging out the
washing. Bartholomew wanted to play.
"In a minute, Ba," said George.
"I'm busy now. In a minute,
then we'll play."

George was sweeping.
Bartholomew got in the way.
He wanted to play.

"IN A

MINUTE!"

George said in a big voice.
"Wait until I've finished."

Bartholomew waited and waited.
He waited and he waited.

George was very busy.

Then at last, George had finished his work.
"I can play now, Ba," he said.

"What shall we play? On the swing…?
With your toys…? I know, hide and seek!"

"Nah, nah, nah," said Bartholomew.

Bartholomew fetched his little red cart
and took George to the woodpile.
He wanted to play …
carrying logs.

He wanted to play …
bringing in the washing.

He wanted to play … sweeping the floor.

"Played enough now, Ba?" George asked.

"Nah!" said Bartholomew.

George fetched the picnic basket.
"Shall we have our picnic now," he asked,
"or in a minute?"

"Nah!" said Bartholomew.

So George and Bartholomew
had their picnic.

"What a busy day we've had," said George.
"You've been such a help, Ba.
Why don't we have a little rest now
and we'll … clear up … in a…"